D1810931

Published in 2022 by BOTH Publishing.

The author asserts their moral right to be identified as the author of their work, in accordance with the Copyright, Designs and Patents Act, 1988.

A CIP catalogue record of this book is available from the British Library.

ISBN - 978-1-913603-16-8
eBook available - ISBN - 978-1-913603-17-5

Printed by Ingram Spark.
Distributed by BOTH Publishing.

Cover design by Alistair Sims & Chrissey Harrison. Coin image by sharpner, licensed via Shutterstock. Typeset by Chrissey Harrison.

Part of the Dyslexic Friendly Quick Reads Project.

www.booksonthehill.co.uk

SILVER
FOR SILENCE

A Philocles Story

J.M. Alvey

Other dyslexic friendly quick read titles from BOTH publishing

Blood Toll

Sharpe's Skirmish

Six Lights off Green Scar

The House on the Old Cliffs

Ultrasound Shadow

The Clockwork Eyeball

Anchor Point

At Midnight I Will Steal Your Soul

Sherlock Holmes and the
Four Kings of Sweden

The Man Who Would Be King

Foreword

By Peter James

Back in 2010 I wrote my first *Quick Reads* novella, *THE PERFECT MURDER*. This was written as adult fiction but with no long words, and was aimed at people who struggled in some way with literacy.

I was lucky enough to win the *Reader's Favourite Award*. At the reception, I was approached by a lady in her late 50s who was close to tears. She told me my novella was the first book she had ever read that was not written for children. For years she had been too embarrassed ever to read in public – on a beach, a park or a bus or a train – because the only stories she was able to cope with were children's books.

Looking at the dyslexic friendly books BOTH published last year I can see how the larger spacing between the words and larger print create an easy-to-read and accessible format without detracting from the narrative journey. I am excited to be part of their project as it is thanks to initiatives such as the work BOTH is doing, that the condition of dyslexia is now catered for in fiction, and people, such as the lady I met, can hold her head up and read in public, like so many other ordinary people.

Silver for Silence

There are two sorts of caller when you're a writer. There are the ones who turn up when you can't write the words down fast enough to keep up with the muse at your shoulder. You're desperate to get rid of those visitors before the fickle nymph flounces off to find someone who appreciates a gift of divine inspiration. Then there are the ones you invite in and offer olives and wine, even if they've only called to return a borrowed bucket. That's because you're desperate for some distraction from an obstinately blank sheet of papyrus and the ink that's been drying on your pen nib.

I wasn't quite at that point, but I certainly looked up with interest when a hesitant knuckle knocked on our gate. My Phrygian slave Kadous went to see who was out in the lane, and he opened the gate wider to allow the visitor in. He didn't have to ask if I was at home to the son of one of Athens' richest men. A writer for hire is always willing to see potential paymasters. Add to that, I like and respect Aristarchos Phytalid, and we've worked together to see justice done a couple of times now. My guest was his youngest son, seven or so years my junior? I didn't find Hipparchos as irritating as I used to, but he still had a long way to go before he was in with a chance of earning my respect. No amount of money can buy that.

"Hipparchos Aristarchou." I rose from my seat in the shade of the porch that runs across the front of my little house. "Good day to you."

"Good day, Philocles Hestaiou." The young man was breathless and red-faced. That might have been from the walk here through the hottest afternoon hours of this late summer's day. Aristarchos and his family live in a substantial, luxurious house in an exclusive district in the heart of Athens, between the agora and the Acropolis. My home is out in Alopeke, well beyond the city walls. Houses here are cheap enough for those of us who can't rely on family income from property across Attica. I wondered what had prompted Hipparchos to hike all this way.

"Please take a seat," I invited him with

a gesture. "Kadous, some well-watered wine for our guest."

"What?" Hipparchos stared at me as if I'd just offered him an egg fresh from the hen coop or something else equally inexplicable. Then he remembered the manners he had been taught. "Thank you. That's very kind."

He didn't sit down though. While Kadous was mixing a measure of wine into a jugful of the water he'd fetched from the local fountain at dawn, Hipparchos paced back and forth across our small courtyard. Our chickens, sitting in the shade of the porch, watched him with beady eyes.

No, I decided, he hadn't caught the sun walking out here without a hat. Hipparchos was agitated about something.

What had the young idiot done now? Before I could work out how to ask that more diplomatically, he turned to me with a question of his own.

"Forgive me, I'm interrupting your work. What are you writing at the moment?"

I could see he was just making small talk, as the well-born are brought up to do, but I answered him anyway.

"I'm roughing out a few ideas for my Lenaia play." The midwinter festival and its drama competition might be months away yet, but I would need to start rehearsals pretty soon. I had already lined up three of my favourite actors for the speaking parts, and they were sending me suggestions for singers to audition for the chorus. What I needed now was some words for them all. Unfortunately, ideas that had seemed promising earlier were evaporating like spilled water on hot paving now that I took a closer look.

Kadous came over with the wine jug and two pottery cups. I cleared away my writing things so he could put everything on the table. We exchanged a glance. Hipparchos was his mother's son when it came to treating slaves as if they were as deaf and dumb as a house's gateposts. If he was hesitating about admitting what he'd done in front of my loyal Phrygian, the young fool must have done something spectacularly stupid.

Kadous walked past Hipparchos, heading across the courtyard. He went into his own quarters beside the gate and closed the door. Hipparchos looked at the three doors opening into the porch from the house behind me.

"Is your – Zosime – is she keeping well?"

We're not married, since my beloved's not an Athenian, so she hardly merited the courtesy of such an enquiry, certainly not in well-born circles. What Hipparchos really wanted to know was where she might be before he confessed whatever had brought him here. All the same, I appreciated him not calling her by one of the less than flattering terms that his rich young idiot friends would have used. Even if that was only because he knew he needed my help.

"She's very well, thank you for asking. She's at work in the city." The women Hipparchos mixes with have no need to earn a living, but Zosime is as talented as she is beautiful, and she paints some of the finest vases you will ever see. She and her potter father share a workshop in the Kerameikos district with a dozen or so other resident foreigners.

I poured wine for us both. "Come and sit down out of the sun."

Hipparchos stood motionless for a moment and then nodded. As he sat on a stool beside my bench, his shoulders slumped. He looked desperately worried. I handed him a cup of wine and waited for him to speak.

He drew a deep breath and poured the first sip of his wine as a libation.

"As blessed Athena is my witness, what I have to tell you is the absolute truth."

I poured an offering to the goddess myself. "May she grant me the wisdom to help you. What's the problem?"

"A man accosted me in the street this morning, not far from home." The echo of Hipparchos' indignation quickly faded. "He said I had to pay my gambling debts, or else he'd go to my father and get the money from him."

"How much are we talking about?" I asked, as neutrally as I could.

"Nothing," he protested. "I have no debts, not from gambling or anything else. I swear to Hermes. You have to believe me!" He was shaking so much that he sloshed more wine from his cup in an inadvertent libation to the god of chance.

I nodded. "I believe you. Drink that before you spill the rest of it."

The thing is, I did believe him. For a start, Hipparchos wouldn't risk anyone going to his father to accuse him of something so dishonourable. A while ago, the young fool got mixed up in a conspiracy that would have disgraced his whole family if the truth had got out. Aristarchos threatened to send him into exile for the rest of his life unless the boy told us what we needed to know to put things right. He wasn't bluffing, Aristarchos, I mean. As it was, Hipparchos had been banished from the city for several months, to sit in a remote house on a family estate and think about what he'd done. From everything I'd seen and heard since, he had learned his lesson.

"Are you sure you're the man the debt collector was looking for? Could there be some mistake?"

Hipparchos drained his cup and shook his head. "He called me by name. He knew where I lived."

"How much money are we talking about?"

"Two hundred drachmae."

"Two hundred?" I nearly spilled my own wine.

A labourer can hope to earn a drachma a day, thanks to Pericles persuading the Council to finance the new temples and fine civic buildings that are going up across the city. I do rather better than that most years, writing people's letters, legal speeches and poems for weddings and funerals, but we were still talking about three month's decent income, give or take.

"I don't know where I'm supposed to get it." Hipparchos went to take another drink and was surprised to find his cup was empty. "My allowance is so meagre these days."

He had the honesty to look embarrassed rather than indignant. We both knew Aristarchos had decided the best way to keep his youngest son out of trouble was to keep him short of spare coin to go drinking with his idiot friends.

I didn't bother asking what he considered a meagre allowance. "You're willing to pay up, even though this isn't your debt? All right then, what will you do the next time this man turns up?"

"Why would he come back? If I paid…" Hipparchos stared at me.

I realised he really must be terrified by the thought of this man, whoever he was, going to his father. Otherwise he would have seen for himself how this fable would play out. I know I call him an idiot, but that's not strictly speaking fair. Hipparchos isn't particularly stupid. He's just lived a very sheltered and privileged life.

I poured him some more wine, and drank my own. "Why has this man come to you, when we both know you don't owe anyone this money? I can think of a couple of reasons. Let's suppose he knows full well there isn't any debt, but he's seeing if you can be scared into paying up regardless. If you hand over that much coin, he's bound to come back to see if he can get a second slice of cheese. On the other hand, maybe he believes you really do owe this money, because somebody somewhere is giving your name when he's playing dice or betting on chariot races. If you pay up now, the next time that imposter loses, you'll have this debt collector straight back on your doorstep."

"Shit." Hipparchos looked as if I'd just emptied the bucket of water from the fountain over his head.

"Right. So let's find out what we're

dealing with."

"How?" Now Hipparchos focused on the problem instead of dreading what his father might say.

"We need to know who this man is, the one who came up to you in the street. You say he called you by name. Did he say, "Oy, Hipparchos Aristarchou!" Or did he see you leave the house and ask if you were Hipparchos Aristarchou?"

He thought for a moment. "He came up to me and said, 'You're Hipparchos Phytalid, aren't you?' I was hardly about to deny it."

"He used your family name?" Only well-born families, and that generally means the wealthy, celebrate their descent from some revered ancestor. In this case, Phytalos was the lucky man who received the very first fig tree from Demeter. The rest of us get by just saying who our father is, along with our voting district as a citizen, to help people place us.

My next question was obvious. "Did he give you his name?"

Hipparchos shook his head. "And I never thought to ask," he admitted ruefully.

"Was there anything you particularly remember about him? An accent? Some mannerism?" I'm always on the lookout for quirks I can use to make a character in a comedy distinctive. Actors need more than a mask and a costume to work with, if a play is going to win.

"No. He was just an ordinary Athenian." Hipparchos was mystified by my question.

I should have expected that. A wealthy young man sees himself as the protagonist taking centre stage. He pays no attention to the chorus coming and going around him.

"Oh well." I grimaced. "I don't suppose just knowing what he calls himself would help us much."

I was hardly going to visit the treasurer of every district brotherhood to see if they recognised some name. Besides, there was no saying this man was even a citizen. There are plenty of neatly dressed slaves with Athenian accents, and even foreigners who've been residents here for years.

"So what do you think?" Hipparchos prompted. His fear of his father's wrath was fading now he had an ally.

"If someone is trying to shake some coin loose with empty threats, the sons of well-born families are obvious targets. If someone wants to get into dice games where they wouldn't usually be welcome, or to convince someone to take their bets, the Phytalid name would certainly open doors."

"So which is it? How do we find out what's going on?" Hipparchos was mystified.

"We find out who this man is, first of all," I said briskly, "and we see what that tells us. While I'm doing that, you go and see your well-born friends. Ask if any strangers have come up to them on the street lately, demanding money they don't owe."

I could see he wanted to object, and I spoke over him mercilessly. "You can't come with me. He knows what you look like. I can't go asking your friends personal questions about unpaid debts. They'll just tell me to piss off. Now, he must have told you where to take this money, and when. What did he say?"

Hipparchos looked a bit sulky, but he couldn't argue with anything I'd said. "He told me to meet him tomorrow at noon, at the temple of Olympian Zeus. He told me to come alone, just bringing the money."

I nodded. "Right, I'll get there an hour or so beforehand. You meet this bloke as arranged, and then you leave.

You can go and ask your friends if they've been asked for money. I'll follow this debt collector back to wherever he came from. You and I can meet up later in the agora, in the Painted Colonnade. I'll see you there at the ninth hour of the day."

"But what do I say to him?" Hipparchos was looking apprehensive again.

I gave that some thought. "Tell him you need a little more time to get that much coin together. Just a couple of days. Remind him you can hardly ask your father for the keys to his strongbox. Set up another meeting."

"Why?" Hipparchos wanted to know. "What are we going to do then?"

"I have no idea," I said bluntly. "That depends on what we find out tomorrow. I just like the idea of knowing where we can find this bloke again if we need to."

Actually, I had a few ideas about what we might do, but I wasn't going to discuss that just yet. The less Hipparchos knew, the less he could give away, even by accident. I'm a writer for hire to pay my way, but I write for the great drama festivals whenever I get the chance. That means I know plenty of actors, and believe me, I knew Hipparchos had no great talent for pretence.

"I suppose so." He drank his wine. "What now?"

"Now you go home. Stay home, and tell Mus to tell any callers he doesn't know that you're not there." No one would get past the enormous Phytalid door slave. Though I didn't think this man would bother Hipparchos again today. I hoped he thought he had his fish good and netted and he'd haul him out of the water tomorrow.

"Oh, yes." Something else occurred to me. "You had better be carrying something that could be the money when you come to the temple. If this is extortion pure and simple, and he sees you arrive empty-handed, my guess is he won't come near you. He'll think you've decided to call his bluff, and who knows, you might have brought a few friends to stand witness when you confront him. Citizens who could testify in court if you prosecute him. He won't risk that."

"For an honest man, you're very good at thinking like a criminal," Hipparchos said wryly.

I didn't take offence. "A good playwright knows to look at a situation from every angle."

Hipparchos stood up. "Thank you for your help," he said stiffly.

I think I managed to hide my surprise. "You're welcome. Whoever's doing this is trying to steal from you and your family. That's an offence against gods and men."

Strictly speaking, I was doing this first and foremost for Aristarchos' sake, but I saw no reason to say that right now. I whistled for Kadous instead. After he'd shown Hipparchos out through the gate,

I spread out my papyrus, pens and ink
and made a few notes to get my thoughts
in order. I wasn't thinking about a play
for the Lenaia drama contest any more.

The sun sank lower and the light
turned golden. Kadous walked into Athens
to escort Zosime safely back home. I
opened the gate when I heard their
voices out in the lane. Zosime stepped up
to put her arms around my neck and kiss
me.

"How are you getting on with the
play?"

I looked at Kadous, who just shrugged.
Of course, he wouldn't have said anything
to her without my permission, even
though he probably heard most of what
had been said.

"Hipparchos paid me a visit." I led Zosime to the bench in the porch and mixed some wine while Kadous served supper for us all. We ate barley bread, salad leaves and beans mashed with herbs and garlic, while I told my beloved about the man who'd come demanding money for a non-existent debt. I told her everything, including the meeting arranged for tomorrow. We have no secrets.

"That's a very public place to be carrying a big bag of silver." Zosime frowned. "And it's a long walk for Hipparchos. Surely there are places closer to his home where they could meet?"

She was right, I realised. "Whoever this is could be planning to rob him on his way there, couldn't they?"

Athens has its share of cloak snatchers and street thieves. That's why Kadous or Zosime's father walks her to and from the workshop. Had some lowlife devised a clever scheme to guarantee whoever he clubbed on the head was definitely worth robbing? Was there more than one lowlife involved? That was enough money to pay two or three men for their time and trouble.

I looked at Kadous. "Can you follow him from the Phytalid house to the temple? Without him or anyone else seeing? Unless he's attacked, of course. Then do whatever you can."

Kadous nodded, confident he could handle any trouble that came his way. It may be a decade and more since he carried my gear as I marched off to war to serve Athens as every citizen should, but he's still extremely handy in a fight.

"Maybe I should come with you..." I shook my head. "No, I need to be at the temple, to keep watch for anyone arriving to meet him. If Hipparchos doesn't get there by noon?" I sighed. "We should have agreed on a route for him to take."

I really wished I'd thought of this earlier. Then I could have told Hipparchos to make sure that whatever he was carrying was heavy enough to be used as a weapon.

"Why don't I follow Kadous?" Zosime suggested. "I'll stay well out of the way, I promise, unless something happens. Then I'll come straight to the temple and find you."

I hesitated. I didn't like the idea of her being anywhere near a fight, but not as much as I disliked the idea of me standing around like a spare phallus at a festival, not knowing what was going on. "I suppose so."

Zosime looked at me. "So how did you get on with the play today?"

I wrinkled my nose. "Not so well."

We spent the rest of the evening tossing ideas back and forth like players in a ball game. Unfortunately everything landed on the floor.

The next morning, I walked into the city with Zosime and Kadous. We went our separate ways pretty much as soon as the young soldiers on guard let us through the Itonian Gate. The other two had a lot further to go than me. I only had to walk through the Limnai district to reach the temple of Olympian Zeus.

Like every other Athenian, I'd been wondering what Pericles was going to do with the unfinished shrine. The tyrant Peisistratos had demolished the greatest of the god's ancient sanctuary in order to glorify himself by building the biggest temple our city had ever seen. The tyrant's sons demolished that, determined to outdo their father, but almighty Zeus had evidently had enough of that family's arrogance. The Peisistratids had been overthrown before more than a handful of columns had gone up and Athens became a democracy. Pericles decided to leave everything well alone, to serve as a reminder to honour the gods with humility.

Even so, the temple precinct is still sacred ground, so there were a fair few people here to seek some blessing or guidance from Zeus. Some of these men and women would be citizens, others resident foreigners and visitors, and doubtless there were some slaves as well. Everyone was speaking the same language, give or take a few dialects, and we were all dressed much the same.

I fit right in as I clasped my hands in a prayerful manner and strolled along the side of the roughly finished temple platform. As I gazed up at the sky, hopefully any onlookers would think I was communing with the great god. I'm not going to lie, I did take the opportunity to respectfully ask if he could give his daughter Thalia, the divine muse of comedy, a nudge to send her in my direction. Then I concentrated on the task that had brought me here.

By the time Hipparchos appeared, I had made a couple of circuits. I had a good idea of who else was already here, so I soon spotted the man heading straight towards him. Hipparchos was right. There was nothing noteworthy about him. He was just another bearded Athenian in a tunic and sandals, maybe a few years older than me. What did catch my eye was the glance the debt collector gave another man. Then he gave that younger man the briefest of nods, before he waved a hand to attract Hipparchos' attention.

I assessed this unexpected second player as quickly and discreetly as I could. He was younger than me, much the same age as Hipparchos. He definitely didn't want Hipparchos to see him. He circled around to make sure he was always standing behind the young Phytalid. That meant I definitely wanted to know who he was, and what his role was in this little drama.

All the same, I turned my back on him. I needed to see what happened when the debt collector found out that bag Hipparchos was carrying wasn't full of silver.

"No trouble so far." Kadous arrived at my side, along with Zosime. Occasionally timing in real life works as smoothly as it does in the theatre.

"Look behind me," I said quietly to them both. "There's a young man who's very interested in whoever Hipparchos is meeting. Can you watch him for me, please?"

Zosime quickly moved to stand facing me, as if we were having a conversation. Kadous stood a few paces away, playing the patiently waiting slave, idly glancing around.

"He's not alone," Zosime observed a moment later. "A couple of others have joined him. He's pointing Hipparchos out."

"Do they look like they're here to cause trouble?" I asked, incredulous. How stupid would you have to be, to offend great Zeus by starting a fight in this sacred space?"

"No." Kadous answered me. "They're just watching and waiting. I'd say two of them don't really know why they're here."

"How's Hipparchos getting on?" Zosime wanted to know.

"Hard to say." I hoped the young idiot wasn't about to wreck the plan we'd agreed.

He didn't look as if he was begging for more time to pay. His jabbing forefinger made me think he was telling the debt collector he could have his money in a few days or not at all. Finally, Hipparchos untied the drawstring of the leather bag he was holding. He poured what looked like pebbles out onto the ground, threw the bag down after them, and stalked away. The debt collector was left staring after him, open-mouthed.

Then he looked in our direction. I looked at Zosime to avoid catching the man's eye. "Hipparchos has gone off in a huff. What do our audience make of that?"

"I'd say the one who was watching first is absolutely furious. The three who came up later?" She paused. "They just look confused."

"What do we do now?" Kadous glanced casually at the debt collector and then over towards the other people who'd been so interested in this meeting. "That lot look ready to leave."

The debt collector was already

heading off. I made a swift decision. "We have to follow them both. Zosime, you come with me. Kadous, see if you can track that nosy young crow back to his nest. Find us in the agora when we meet Hipparchos, if you can. If not, we'll see you back at home."

I didn't wait for the Phrygian to answer me. Zosime and I had to get moving if we were going to stay on the debt collector's trail. She slipped her arm through mine and we hurried off like a couple who'd just remembered they'd forgotten an appointment with the city's tax gatherers. I was glad she wasn't hampered by the long pleated gown that a citizen woman would be wearing. Her draped dress was knee-length, like my tunic.

"Can you see Hipparchos anywhere?" I realised we were heading in the direction he had just gone. Though that wasn't so surprising. This was the fastest route back to the city's centre.

"No." After peering ahead, Zosime snatched a glance over her shoulder. "Our new friend is coming this way too, along with his friends."

"Where do you suppose they're going?" I wondered aloud, frustrated. "If the two of them are in this together, why didn't they discuss their next steps after Hipparchos walked away?"

"Because they couldn't do that with those other three listening in." Zosime worked out the answer as quickly as me, along with the next obvious question. "So what were they doing there?"

"They were supposed to be witnesses," I realised. "To see Hipparchos handing over a big bag of money to someone. That's why the so-called debt collector wanted to meet him in such a public space."

I'd been thinking about that, ever since Zosime had first mentioned it seemed odd. I'd decided it was to reassure Hipparchos that he wasn't going to be beaten and robbed in some back alley. Now I was thinking I might be wrong about that.

"This might not be about Hipparchos at all," I said uneasily. "What if someone's trying to use the stupid boy to discredit Aristarchos?"

Not every rich man in Athens deserves to be called one of the great and good.

For every prosperous citizen who takes his obligations seriously, and does his duty in the courts and the Council, there'll be another who thinks his wealth should mean he's above the law. These men ship their strongboxes off to temples outside Athens for safekeeping. Then they can plead poverty when they're called on to bear the costs of a new trireme or a festival contest, to repay the gods for their good fortune. They lie and connive to make themselves even richer, and they don't care what their deceits cost other people. These men had been behind the treachery that Hipparchos got himself mixed up in.

My blood ran cold despite the heat of the day. "If they have witnesses – citizen witnesses – who can stand up in court and swear they saw Hipparchos handing over that much money, he won't be able to deny it. Then it'll be his word against whatever that lowlife says the silver was for." I kept my eyes fixed on the so-called debt collector as the streets got busier. "If they bring up the conspiracy Nikandros dragged him into, Hipparchos' word won't be worth an eighth of an obol."

And all the effort Aristarchos and I had gone to would be exposed. His enemies would make it look as if he only cared about saving his idiot son's neck. How many people would listen when we tried to explain how close Athens had come to calamity?

"Why go to all this trouble?" Zosime was sceptical. "They could just post a notice in the agora, announcing someone was taking Hipparchos to court over an unpaid debt."

"They'd have to convince a magistrate there was a case to answer." I objected.

"Do you think someone who's ready to lie about Hipparchos before a court wouldn't be prepared to tell lies to get him there?" Zosime countered. "Besides, it wouldn't matter that much if the case was thrown out. As soon as an official notice was put up for people to read, the gossip would do plenty of damage."

I couldn't argue with any of that. Rumour runs around the agora faster than the wind. Even so, I was convinced there was more to this than trying to trick a bag of silver out of a rich young idiot. But I needed to concentrate on following the so-called debt collector. The Acropolis loomed up ahead of us, and there were several different routes he could take.

"Where's he going?" Zosime wondered a little while later.

We were approaching the junction where the road that heads off to the theatre of Dionysos meets the one that goes north to curl around the Acropolis. Like me, Zosime had been expecting the debt collector to take that second route. I expected we'd soon be passing through the agora to get to the Kerameikos district where gamblers hang out in and around the brothels.

Instead, he was taking the other road. We followed him past the theatre and through the streets overlooked by the south-facing crags of the Acropolis. When I got the chance, I looked back to see if his young co-conspirator was heading this way as well. There was no sign of him, which was a relief. I didn't want to have to try explaining ourselves if the two of them challenged us. On the other hand, that meant I had no idea where that mystery man had gone. I could only hope Kadous was still on his trail, and that he hadn't been spotted. A slave confronted by four indignant citizens would be in a whole lot of trouble.

The man we were following kept up a steady pace. We headed into the heart of the Kollytos district where some of Athens' wealthiest families live. The streets grew quieter, because rich men buy tall, muscular slaves to guard their gates. They're ready to challenge anyone who might look curious about what was on the other side of the tall, blank walls that surround those big houses.

I started to feel conspicuous, and I was even more concerned that someone was going to ask Zosime what business she had here. She wasn't dressed like a citizen and there was no point in pretending she was one, even if doing that wasn't illegal. As soon as my beloved opened her mouth, it would be obvious she'd grown up in Crete.

Suddenly, Zosime slowed down. Her arm through mine made me do the same. I saw what she had realized. Our debt collector – though I was pretty sure by now he was no such thing – had reached his destination. He stopped outside a solid, well-made gate. As he knocked, presumably someone inside slid open the grille to see who was out there. He was allowed in at once, and the gate closed behind him.

"That doesn't look like a gambling den to me," I remarked.

"Maybe it's where whoever owns the gambling den lives?" But Zosime sounded sceptical.

"Let's see if our man comes out again after delivering his message. Then we can see where he goes next."

We waited and we watched, but the gate stayed obstinately closed.

"So who lives there? How, by all the gods above and below, do we find out?" I looked around, frustrated.

What I needed was someone who'd share some local gossip in exchange for me buying whatever they might be selling.

Unfortunately, the centre of Kollytos doesn't have a tavern on every other street corner. It isn't a district where the locals head out for an acceptable jug of wine and a meal at a fair price if they don't fancy whatever their slave found in the market that day. Fine vintages are delivered to these houses in amphorae by the cartload and they have whole rooms set aside for cooking, not a charcoal brazier in the corner of the courtyard. Slaves would be sent out at dawn to buy the best and freshest the farmers' stalls had to offer, and again in the afternoon, to be ready when the bell in the agora announced the day's fish were being brought up from Piraeus.

I sighed. "I suppose we can watch and wait for a little while longer. If someone else comes out, we can follow them to – to wherever they're going. Maybe we can find someone to ask a few questions."

Someone who wouldn't immediately tell their wealthy patron that some scruffy stranger was being nosy? That hope was as thin as one of Odysseus' men, when they were trapped and starving on the isle of Thrinacia, but I couldn't think of anything else.

"Remember you agreed to meet Hipparchos in the agora," Zosime reminded me. "In the Painted Colonnade at the ninth hour."

"I remember." I looked around, but there were no sundials anywhere to be seen. I checked the sun in the sky and the shadows and reckoned we still had a fair amount of time in hand. "Let's find somewhere cooler."

There was a side street not too far away where we found some shade and we could still see that mysterious gate. No one appeared to accuse us of loitering. No one appeared at all. We waited, and we waited some more. I started to get uncomfortably thirsty.

To take my mind off that, I started to think about going up to the gate and knocking on it myself. If I simply asked who lived there, the door slave might share that much information before telling me to get lost. He might not chase after me, if I ran off instead of answering when he asked me who I was and why I wanted to know. Of course, a house like that probably had spare slaves he could send after me. Slaves who might catch Zosime as well. If not, she'd have to head for the agora alone, while I... I had no idea what I would do.

"What's that?" Zosime's ears were sharper than mine.

I heard the rhythmic tread of several people carrying something heavy between them. The sound was coming from somewhere beyond the gate we were watching, where the street curved around. We stayed of sight as best we could, and waited. We didn't have to wait long. A curtained litter appeared carried by six strapping slaves. The sort of thing that some of Athens' wealthiest women use when they're calling on their friends and relations, to avoid having to walk the same streets as the rest of us.

Only some of the wealthy use them. That sort of Persian luxury still gets filthy looks from Athenians whose grandfathers died fighting the bastards at Marathon. Plenty of other people have lost fathers, brothers and sons, killed in the battles the bastards provoked through the decades that followed. That's something Hipparchos and I do have in common. Our eldest brothers both died when Athenian forces were sent to help the Egyptians revolt against Persian rule. But we're not supposed to hold grudges as long as the peace that Callias finally brokered still holds.

"What is it? What's the matter?" Zosime must have seen something in my face.

It wasn't that old sorrow. I'd recognised those slaves, and that litter. I watched as the gate opened and they were welcomed inside. I ran a hand through my curls, more baffled than anything else.

"That litter? It belongs to Aristarchos' wife."

Zosime stared at me. "What is she doing here?"

I shrugged helplessly. "I have no idea."

The gate closed with a bang that echoed down the empty street.

I held out my hand to Zosime. "Let's get to the agora."

We headed for the Acropolis and followed the Panathenaic Way to the bustling centre of our great city. It's not only the most important of all Athens' marketplaces. The traders and entertainers are surrounded by statues that celebrate our democracy's heroes, and there are any number of shrines to the gods and goddesses who watch over us. Official notices from the Council and the courts are posted on whitewashed boards, and travelling tutors sit in the shady colonnades to lecture anyone who'll listen and pay a few obols for the privilege. When I'm not writing a play, I'll sit on the colonnade steps with my fellow writers for hire, to watch the world go by while we wait for work.

That means I know the best of the

wine sellers who set up their carts around the edge of the agora. I paid Elpis an obol for a generous measure of well-mixed wine and two rough pottery cups. We headed for the steps of the Painted Colonnade, where dramatic pictures celebrate Hellas' triumphs from the fall of Troy onwards. Zosime and I were both more interested in quenching our thirst, though I made sure to offer the first sip to Hermes. We definitely needed a few favours from the god of luck, if we were going to untangle this mystery.

I looked at the bold red letters on the court notices and glanced at Zosime. "What do you think about suggesting Hipparchos dares whoever's demanding this money to prosecute him for an unpaid debt? We'd have to go to Aristarchos first, but we might learn something about who's behind this."

She pursed her lips. "More likely they'll scurry for cover like cockroaches when someone opens a storeroom door. That'll be the last he sees of them."

"Which would at least put an end to this nonsense." I wondered if that might be for the best.

Zosime wasn't convinced. "Do you really think so? If Hipparchos' mother is somehow involved?"

"How could she be?" I broke off as I saw he was approaching us. "Let's talk about that later. When we know what Kadous has to tell us. Maybe he's found the blade that'll cut through this knot."

"Good afternoon." Hipparchos arrived and sat down on the steps beside me.

"Do you want to get yourself something to drink?" I gestured in Elpis' direction.

He waved that away. "I'm fine. So how did you get on?"

"We followed the man you met to a private house in Kollytos, so I really don't think he's a legitimate debt collector. What did you learn from your friends?" I asked before he could ask me to elaborate.

"I've asked everyone I can think of, and no one has been accosted by someone demanding money." Hipparchos hugged his knees. "No one could make any sense of it."

"What did the man say, when you said he'd have to wait for his money?" Zosime enquired.

Hipparchos frowned. "He didn't seem to know what to say. I expected him to threaten me again, but he said he was willing to wait. We agreed to meet there at noon again, the day after tomorrow. Is that all right?"

I nodded, and chose my next words carefully. "So it doesn't look like this is mistaken identity, and no one else is being menaced by chancers. That means someone is picking on you specifically, but you've been keeping your nose clean, so they've had to make up this story of you owing money. Do you think someone could be trying to provoke you into doing something unwise, to make trouble for your father? Is he involved in drafting any new laws or proposals for the Council that someone might not like? Has he had any business disputes lately?"

I silently thanked Athena that Aristarchos had decided to make sure Hipparchos understood his family name came with obligations as well as unearned advantages. He was involving him in such discussions these days.

The lad looked blank. "No, I mean, he's as busy as he usually is, but things are going smoothly as far as I know. And I really have been staying out of trouble," he insisted, before we could ask.

"I believe you." I got to my feet. "Let's call it a day. We'll see what we can find out about this house in Kollytos tomorrow."

Hipparchos stood up as well. "I'll call on you first thing in the morning."

"We'll see you then." I watched him walk away, and then offered my hand to Zosime who was still sitting on the steps.

"You've got some cunning plan to get past that gate?" She stood up and brushed dust off her skirt.

"No," I admitted. "I really hope Kadous has found a scent for us to follow. If he hasn't, I don't know what we're going to do."

We walked back to our little house in Alopeke. Since I had the key to the gate, we found Kadous sitting in the shade outside, swapping jokes with Sosistratos' slave from down the lane.

"How long have you been waiting?"

I opened up and we went into the courtyard. "Why didn't you come to find us in the agora?"

I could see he'd visited a market somewhere, since he was carrying fresh bread and some cheese.

Kadous put everything down on the porch table. "I needed to speak to you first, without Hipparchos around."

"Why?" Something in his voice made me uneasy. "Where did the man who wanted those witnesses go?"

"The four of them went to a tavern in Diomea, where they met up with a whole lot of others. They hadn't been there very long when Hipparchos arrived." He looked at me. "It was obvious they all know each other."

I stared at him. What was going on? Well, I had until the morning to work out how to ask Hipparchos that.

><<

When I say that Zosime paints pottery, I'm not talking about the bold black and red wine bowls or water jugs with gods and heroes striding across them. She specialises in the narrow ewers for wine and oil that have far more personal decoration on their white sides. Since these are mostly used for making offerings to the dead, she's become very skilled at painting a portrait of a lost loved one from their family's description. She can draw the likeness of someone she's actually seen with a few strokes of a pen.

By the time Hipparchos knocked on our gate the following morning, she had given me deft sketches of the four youths who'd watched his encounter at the temple of Zeus. After I'd welcomed Hipparchos in, we sat at the table in the porch. Kadous and Zosime had already walked into the city.

"So what have you found out?" Hipparchos asked as soon as his backside hit the stool.

I offered him the first sheet of papyrus. That was the portrait of the man we'd identified as the leader of that little chorus at the shrine. "Do you know who this is?"

"Meniskos Architimou. Why do you want to know about him?"

"Does he happen to live in Kollytos?" I asked, as casually as I could.

Hipparchos shook his head. "Diomea."

"How about any of these?" I showed him the other pictures. "Do you know them, and where they live?"

"I know them all." He tapped one. "This is Gorgias Dionysodorou. He lives in Kollytos."

"Is his family particularly friendly with yours?"

Hipparchos narrowed his eyes at me, to let me know he knew I was being evasive. He answered all the same.

"I would say we're more acquaintances than friends, but my mother and his have been visiting each other recently. I think she might be considering one of Gorgias' brothers as a possible husband for my sister Epicharis. They're Medontids."

So, very well-born indeed, descended from Medon, the first archon of Athens back when magistracies were hereditary. One way the well-born stay so rich is they marry their sons and daughters to each other. That definitely helps keep coin in the family.

"Right." I was relieved that answered the awkward question of who was in the litter we'd seen.

"Why do you ask?" Hipparchos persisted.

"We saw the four of them at the temple yesterday. They seemed very interested in what you were doing. But if you know them, that's no great surprise.

They must have recognised you." That was true as far as it went.

Hipparchos looked at me for a long moment. "Right. Well then, what did you find out by following that man who was expecting me to hand him a big bag of silver?"

"We know where he lives, and today, we need to find out his name." Once again, I wasn't lying, not exactly. I got to my feet.

Hipparchos did the same. "Let's go then."

I shook my head. "We still can't risk him recognising you."

"So what am I supposed to do?" he protested.

"Go home and wait for us to come

and tell you what we learn. Put in a solid day's work helping your father," I suggested. "If someone is trying to make trouble for him, or for you, let's show anyone who's curious that you're a solidly responsible citizen."

Hipparchos gave me another long, thoughtful look. "All right."

We headed into Athens. Hipparchos didn't want to talk about much of anything on the way, which was a relief. Once we were through the Itonian Gate, we parted company at the first major junction. As I headed for what had to be the Medontid house in Kollytos, I rubbed the head of the Hermes pillar on the corner and prayed briefly for a little good fortune.

I found Kadous loitering in the same side street where Zosime and I had watched the Medontid gate. "Any sign of him?"

"Not yet." Kadous knew I meant the so-called debt collector.

That might be good news or bad, depending on whether or not the man was actually in there. All we could do was wait and see. While we waited, I told Kadous what I'd learned from Hipparchos.

As it turned out, Hermes was smiling on us. It wasn't long before the gate opened and our quarry came out. He headed in the general direction of the agora.

Kadous and I followed, with the

Acropolis soaring ahead of us. Just before he reached the road that would take him to the Panathenaic Way, we sprinted up behind him. When our quarry turned to see what was going on, Kadous didn't stop. As the Phrygian and I had agreed, he ran straight past the so-called debt collector, stopped and turned. Now we had him caught between us.

For the moment, the man looked more puzzled than anything else. I could understand that, now we had got so close. There was nothing about him to catch a street thief's eye. He wasn't carrying anything, and while his sandals and tunic were good quality, they were well-worn cast-offs. Another way the rich stay rich is not spending any money they don't have to on dressing their household slaves.

"Don't say anything," I said briskly. "Just listen. You went to the temple of Olympian Zeus yesterday, expecting to get a bag of silver from Hipparchos Phytalid. You have demanded money from a well-connected citizen with lies and threats. If we take you to the magistrates right now, and I swear to that, your life is as good as over. You'll be tortured until you confess."

I broke off as the man collapsed to his knees. He huddled on the ground and wrapped his arms around his head, weeping with terror. So we were right. This poor wretch was a slave. A slave who had to do what he was told or face dire consequences. A slave who clearly knew that such threats would be carried out. It made no difference that he was tidily dressed with decent sandals to wear. It's not only the slaves you see with bruises and scars who are mistreated. There are plenty of ways to scar a man's mind, or a woman's, or a child's.

I dropped to one knee as he mumbled something incomprehensible. "Please, don't say anything," I begged him. "I really don't want you to tell me what's going on. Then I won't be able to swear to anything in front of a court. I'm going to leave you now, so you can talk to my slave Kadous. I give you my word, as holy Athena is my judge, that I won't allow anyone to question him. No one will ever know we have spoken to you."

I glanced up at the Phrygian. I honestly hadn't expected such a dramatic reaction from the Medontid slave. Kadous nodded and gestured, telling me to go on my way. Reluctantly, I stood up and headed for the Panathenaic Way. I managed to resist the temptation to glance back over my shoulder as I went, so I was one up on Orpheus if nothing else.

When I reached the agora, I didn't stop. I followed the Panathenaic Way to the Kerameikos district, and cut through the alleys that would take me to the pottery where Zosime and her father work. Inside, I found the usual bustle of activity. I grinned at the potters who had looked up, expecting me to be a customer. When they recognised me, they smiled ruefully, and went back to shaping spinning clay with miraculous speed and ease.

Zosime's workbench is against the back wall, and Menkaure has his wheel set up close by. He let the start of some great vase slow to a halt as I reached them, and Zosime set down her paintbrush.

"Well?" Menkaure had heard the story so far, and our plan for the morning, as I had expected.

"We caught up with him easily enough." I found a stool, sat down close to Zosime, and told them both what had just happened. "Now we have to wait and see what Kadous can get out of him. He was scared shitless when we confronted him." I felt really bad about that, though I still couldn't see anything else we could have done.

Menkaure shook his head. "You Athenians. I've never understood what makes you think torturing slaves is the only way to get to the truth."

He's from southern Egypt, and I have no idea what the laws and customs might be there. I didn't ask, and I didn't take offence either. It wasn't as if I had any good reasons to give him. It makes no sense to me either, but that's the law in Athens, so I guess grey-eyed Athena must know what she's doing. Even so, I meant what I'd said to the Medontid wretch. I will never give my permission for Kadous to be questioned like that.

"I need to get this finished." Zosime gave me a quick smile as she picked up her brush again.

I got to my feet. "I'll make myself useful."

Truth be told, I would have struggled to sit still while we waited for Kadous to appear. There was no knowing which way up the coin we had just tossed was going to land. If we saw Athena's face, we would find out what was going on. If it landed owl-side up, we would be as much in the dark as ever. If that happened, I was out of ideas. I'd just have to persuade Hipparchos to take this whole mess to his father.

Meantime, I fetched water from the nearby fountain, and helped the aged Thessalian who stokes the kiln stack a delivery of firewood. A pottery might be very different to my father's leather-goods workshop that my two older brothers run now, but whatever any craftsmen might be doing, there will always be jobs around for idle hands.

As it happened, Kadous appeared pretty quickly. He looked agitated as he headed for Zosime's corner. That couldn't be good. I put down the bucket I was carrying and joined them.

"His mother isn't discussing his sister's marriage," the Phrygian said without any prologue. "She's looking at one of the Medontid daughters as a possible bride for Hipparchos. The thing is, the girl, Glaphyra, she's already in love with Meniskos Architimou."

"Seriously?" I thought every well-born girl understood they'd be marrying to advance their family's interests. They

74

were taught that before they left their nurse's care. Even ordinary citizens like my brothers weigh up the practical advantages of a match when they're attracted to a neighbour's daughter.

Kadous nodded. "Gorgias has been Meniskos' best friend since they first learned their letters together, so he wants to see the two of them married. They came up with this scheme to make Hipparchos look like a bad bet in the husband stakes."

"What do you mean?" Zosime didn't follow.

I did. "They wanted witnesses to see him handing over a big bag of silver for a debt that he didn't even bother disputing. Dionysodoros Medontid won't want to hand over his daughter and her dowry to a man who lets coins slip though his fingers like water."

"But Hipparchos will recognise the man he gave the money to as one of their slaves," Menkaure objected.

"Not if the poor wretch has been sold and shipped off to some city on the other side of the Aegean," I guessed. "They'll get rid of him as soon as Hipparchos is fool enough to hand over the money. Gorgias and Meniskos probably had some scheme to challenge him in front of witnesses about that payment, and then—"

"That doesn't matter now," Kadous interrupted.

I stared at him. I couldn't remember when he'd last done that.

"They've given up that idea after yesterday," he explained. "After Hipparchos asked the rest of their friends if any strangers had demanded money from them."

"So what's the plan now?" I could see from his face that there was more to come. As I say, the well-born seem to think their slaves are deaf and dumb.

Kadous looked grim. "They're going to take Hipparchos out drinking and dose him with henbane. Once he's out of his senses, they'll dump him in a brothel and make sure he's found by one of their other friends, one who has no idea what's going on."

Menkaure shrugged. "What's so bad about that?"

"For a start, those idiots could kill him." Zosime was horrified. "Even doctors only use henbane when there's no other option. If they need to cut someone's leg off, or something."

Menkaure acknowledged the truth of that with a grimace. "I meant, who's going to care if a young man visits a brothel?"

Kadous looked at me. "They're going to bribe the brothel owner to say that Hipparchos isn't a customer. That he goes there to work, because his father keeps him so short of money."

"Oh, shit." That was a very different bowl of beans. That scandal would blacken both their names. The well-born buy sex like anyone else, but they absolutely do not sell their arses in a back-alley whorehouse for two obols a go.

"He's at home at the moment, isn't he?" Zosime asked anxiously.

"I really hope so." I gave her cheek a quick kiss. "We need to warn him."

Kadous and I headed out. We didn't have too far to go. I knocked on the Phytalid household's gate, and Mus who guards the entrance looked through the grille. He knew who I was. When Aristarchos had been sponsoring one of my festival plays, I was a regular visitor.

"Good day to you," I said quickly. "We need to see Hipparchos."

Mus opened the gate, but when I stepped forward, he raised a massive hand. "He's not here."

My heart sank. "Where is he?"

"He went out a while ago with two friends." Mus frowned. He could see we were concerned. He may look as if he was carved out of a mountain, and his barbarian accent would startle a donkey, but he's not stupid.

I rubbed a hand over my beard. "Gorgias Dionysodorou and Meniskos Architimou?"

Mus nodded. "What's wrong?"

"How long ago did they leave?"

"Less than an hour. A lot less. What's wrong?" Mus asked again.

I turned to Kadous. "Did the Medontid slave say which brothel?"

He nodded. "In general terms. I can get us close enough to find it."

Praise be to bright-eyed Athena and

keen-eyed Hermes. I looked at Mus. "I can't explain, not yet."

Kadous was already heading back towards the agora. I hurried after him. I felt sick as I wondered what I might end up having to explain to Aristarchos. I also felt blisteringly angry with Hipparchos. Why couldn't the young idiot just do as he was told?

The Phrygian led the way. Like most slaves who've been with the same family for years, he knows the highways and byways of Athens like the back of his hand. At sometime or other he must have run errands for me or my brothers in every district of the city. Walking fast, we were soon on a road heading north towards the Acharnian Gate.

When we reached the tangle of streets

where the Kerameikos district edges into Skambonidai, Kadous' pace slowed. "It's somewhere around here. Down a side street off this road to the gate."

"If that slave got it right." If he was wrong, I had no idea what we could do.

"He was certain." Kadous had no doubt about that. "He wanted to make amends for what he'd been forced to do."

I looked around, trying to see into any taverns as we passed by. "They'll want to get pretty close before they risk dosing him with henbane, don't you think?"

He nodded. "Let's hope so."

We had both seen army surgeons mixing henbane into their potions as they tried to save wounded men's lives in the bloody aftermath of battle. A skilled doctor could use the herb to send men to sleep or dull their pain until they recovered or they died. Occasionally though, a patient would start raving. These men didn't seem to realise how badly they were wounded, trying to walk on a shattered knee or ripping bandages off a bleeding wound. Sometimes they attacked the doctors who were so desperately trying to help them. Whether the herb would send a man into a stupor or a frenzy was in the gift of the gods.

We walked along the road, pausing to look up every alley and side street. It was another hot late-summer day, but a little further on, I felt a chill. Had Gorgias and Meniskos ever seen a field hospital? I suddenly doubted it. Rich young men whose families can afford the upkeep of horses do their military service in the cavalry. Even when Athens goes to war, they sit around in their saddles on the edge of a battle, waiting for a general's call. Meantime, the rest of us poor bloody hoplites are standing shoulder to shoulder in a shield wall, trying to force the enemy's phalanxes back without getting a spear through the throat or the eye.

Zosime was right. Hipparchos was in very real danger of being poisoned by his idiot so-called friends. And all of this over who got to marry a particular girl? The whole thing was ridiculous.

We passed another side street. I looked down it and was ready to move on when something caught my eye. I took another look. Two men were helping a third to walk away from us. I could see they had their arms around their stumbling friend's waist while his arms were draped over their shoulders. His head lolled forward as if he was drunk. Drunk, or dosed with henbane?

"Down there." I pointed the trio out to Kadous.

"Is that them?"

He had a point. Three men in tunics aren't particularly recognisable from behind. On the other hand, who else could they be?

"We need to find out."

"Fair enough."

We started down the side street. After a few paces, I stopped.

"Wait a moment."

What was going to happen when we confronted Meniskos and Gorgias? I guessed they would dump Hipparchos and run for it. I could grab one of them, but if Kadous tackled the other? A slave who defends himself when he's attacked has nothing much to fear, but a slave who lays a violent hand on an Athenian citizen is in a world of trouble. Add to that, what state was Hipparchos going to be in?

I turned to the Phrygian. "Go and find some Scythians. Go to the city prison if you need to. Wait, on second thoughts, go straight there, as quick as you can. Tell them to bring a doctor."

"Right." Kadous understood. He turned back the way we had come. By the time he reached the main road, he was running.

I went on alone, walking fast enough to close up the distance between me and the trio ahead. Keeping Hipparchos alive was my priority. It didn't matter if his so-called friends ran away. I knew their names and families, and I could testify to seeing them dragging Hipparchos along this street, his limp feet trailing in the dust. Maybe I'd even let them get as far as the brothel. As long as he survived, he could tell the rest of the story. Then Gorgias and Meniskos could try to explain themselves.

If Hipparchos didn't survive? Hopefully the Scythian's doctor would be able to swear that he'd been poisoned by henbane. The Scythians are public slaves, so their doctor could give evidence in court. They can also grab hold of a citizen or anyone else who's disturbing the peace in Athens without any penalty. They only answer to the city magistrates.

I was catching up with the trio fast. Abruptly, I'd had enough. I had to see what had happened to Hipparchos. "Hey, Gorgias! How's your day going?"

I called out a cheery greeting, like someone who'd just seen a friend. The three of them halted. Well, at least the two dragging the third man did. The one on the left glanced over his shoulder. That answered one question at least. I recognised Gorgias.

He had absolutely no idea who I was. "Can I—?"

I never found out what he had been going to ask. Hipparchos drew his feet up to stand solidly on the beaten earth. Since he already had his arms draped around their necks, he hooked his hands around his so-called friends' heads and tried to smack them together. As all three of them spun around, I saw Meniskos get his hands up in time to ward Gorgias off. Even so, his co-conspirator's forehead hit his face with a lot more than a glancing blow. They staggered apart.

Hipparchos went after Gorgias. There was no sign he had been drinking wine or anything else. He grabbed Gorgias around the waist like a wrestler and rammed him hard into the closest wall. Gorgias raised his linked hands high and smacked his fists down hard on Hipparchos' back. Hipparchos swept him off his feet. Now they were on the ground, grappling in the dust.

Meniskos had wasted precious time realising that his nose was bleeding. Now he saw I was coming for him. He turned to run, but someone must have heard this commotion further down the street. A door opened and a curious man stepped out to block his way.

Meniskos spun around and ran back towards me. Long-legged and lithe as an athlete, he jumped over Gorgias' thrashing legs. I braced myself, waiting to see which way he would go to try and get past me. Meniskos jinked from one foot to the other, like a hare trying to dodge pursuing hounds.

He went one way. I went the other. He lengthened his stride, accelerating. I

thrust my fist out straight, bracing myself
as best as I could. He hit my forearm
with his chin. I staggered but I stayed
on my feet. Meniskos' feet were up in
the air, almost level with my shoulder.
If we had been two acrobats, everyone
would be laughing. Acrobats know how
to do things like this without hurting
themselves.

Meniskos was no acrobat. He crashed
to the ground, as flat as a man lying
on a bed. I swear I felt the earth shake
through the soles of my sandals. All
the wind was knocked out of him with
something between a gasp and a groan.
As he lay there, his face twisted in
agony. He could only make a noise like a
wheezing mouse.

I stood there, ready to grab him as

soon as he made any move. Meantime, I looked over to see that Hipparchos had Gorgias pinned, face down. He gripped Gorgias' wrists and twisted his arms up between his shoulder blades. Gorgias yelped, but with Hipparchos' knees on either side of his waist, there was nothing he could do to free himself.

Hipparchos looked at me and grinned. "Thanks for coming to my rescue."

"You seem to be managing fairly well on your own." Though I wasn't at all sure what his plan might have been if they had reached their destination.

"How did you find me?"

"Mus told us you'd gone out with this precious pair. We soon picked up your trail." I was going to be as vague as I could about that. I certainly wasn't going to mention the Medontid slave with these two listening.

"Who's "we"?" Hipparchos asked.

"Me and Kadous." I jerked my head back towards the agora. The city prison is a little way down a road that leaves from the southern side. "He's gone to fetch some Scythians."

Hearing that made Gorgias thrash some more, not that it did him any good. He was right to panic. The Scythians would take this pair to the city prison, and while they'd be released before sunset, that would only happen after their fathers had been informed they had assaulted a fellow citizen without provocation.

Meniskos made a noise like a startled ferret. He was still lying at my feet, unable or unwilling to move. When I looked down at him, he closed his eyes. I wondered how badly he was hurt. I hoped Kadous was able to bring a doctor as well as a few muscular Scythians to take him off our hands.

"What were you thinking?" I asked quickly, before Hipparchos could ask me anything else. "Why go anywhere with these two?"

"To find out what they were up to," he said, as if that was the obvious thing to do. "You obviously weren't going to tell me anything you knew."

"And?" I wondered what these idiots might have confessed.

"They wanted me to drink some wine from a jug they'd brought with them, but I wasn't about to trust anything Gorgias gave me after talking to you this morning." Hipparchos gave his captive's hands a vindictive twist and was rewarded with another yelp. "I pretended to take a few swigs, then I dropped it 'by accident'. I started to play drunk, since I guessed that's what they were expecting. That got them excited, so I played along some more. Once they thought I was too far gone to hear, they started talking about taking me to a brothel where I'd be found out of my wits and playing the whore."

He was angry, and that was fine with me, because it meant he didn't notice this wasn't exactly news to me. Better yet, he could swear to all this in court. No one need ever know the Medontid slave had said a word.

"What are you going to do next?" I asked. "Will you prosecute them for assault?"

Meniskos moaned again, while Gorgias just pressed his face into the dirt.

"That depends on what my father says." Hipparchos looked at me. I don't know what he saw in my face, but he raised his brows. "You don't imagine I'm going to keep this from him? Do you think I'm an idiot?"

There was only one honest answer to that. "Not anymore."

A few days later, I was politely requested to call on Aristarchos Phytalid whenever I might find it convenient.

"I'll come back with you now," I told Ambrakis, the slave who'd brought the message. "Just let me put this away."

I made sure my papyrus sheets were stacked in the right order and the ink on the last one was dry. I'd had plenty of work to keep me busy while I'd been waiting for this summons.

We walked into the city in silence, but from the sidelong glances Ambrakis gave me, I could see that he, and presumably the entire household, were itching to know what I knew. That was understandable, but it wasn't my place to tell them. The head of an Athenian family's authority is absolute within his walls, whether he's descended from a god or a goatherd.

Aristarchos' house has two courtyards. He was sitting in his customary place in the inner one, in a shady corner. As usual he was reading letters concerning his business affairs. He put down the papyrus in his hand and waved me to a stool. "Thank you for coming so promptly."

"It's always a pleasure to see you." I sat down.

"I gather I have you to thank for saving Hipparchos from disgrace once again," he said wryly. "At least he had the sense to go to you instead of trying to find a way out of that labyrinth on his own."

"I was glad to help." I hesitated, but I couldn't help asking. "Meniskos and Gorgias…?"

Aristarchos' smile was as thin as a razor's edge. "I believe Meniskos will be representing his family's interests in Sardinia for the next few years. Gorgias has been sent on some errand to Phoenicia. He is not expected back any time soon."

So there wouldn't be a court case. I guessed Aristarchos had come to some agreement with the fathers of those two young idiots. Discretion would save everyone from embarrassment, including his own son.

"How is Hipparchos?"

Aristarchos sighed. "Annoyed by gossip

around the agora, murmuring he did have unpaid debts or worse. He will just have to rise above it."

I grinned. "That will soon die down."

Aristarchos gave me a measuring look. "Is that so?"

I nodded. "My actors and I must have been overheard talking about my new play for the Lenaia. You know how easily people get the wrong idea in a noisy tavern."

"Really?" Aristarchos had a glint in his eye. "What is this play about?"

"Three young men are rivals for the same bride," I said blandly. "They hatch ridiculous schemes to discredit each other. It's set in a gymnasium."

I'd decided the chorus who give a

play its name would be wrestlers hanging around. That was offering me plenty of scope for the rude jokes Lenaia audiences like.

Aristarchos' lips twitched. "I am surprised. Actors are usually so discreet before a play has been performed."

"There are always rumours." I spread my hands. "What can you do?"

This was as much as I could do, and Hipparchos was still going to have an uncomfortable few months. Once the comedy had been staged though, hopefully people would think any gossip about rich young men doing stupid things was prompted by mistaken memories blurred by festival drinking.

"Shall we have some wine?"

Aristarchos raised a hand, and his slave and secretary Lydis appeared with a tray holding a jug and goblets. "Tell me, how are your brothers faring?"

"Thank you." I took my wine from Lydis, and offered my first sip to Athena.

I'd been making a lot of offerings these past few days, to Athena, to Hermes, to Zeus, and to the muse of comedy, Thalia. I wasn't sure which deity had decided to send Hipparchos my way, to give me this inspiration for my play as I solved his problem, but I was very grateful.

About the Author

J M Alvey studied Classics at Oxford in the 1980s. As an undergraduate, notable achievements in startling tutors included citing the comedic principles of Benny Hill in a paper on Aristophanes, and using military war-gaming rules to analyse and explain apparent contradictions in historic accounts of the Battle of Thermopylae.

Crime fiction has always been relaxation reading and that love of mysteries and thrillers continued through a subsequent, varied career, alongside an abiding fascination with history and the ancient world. She also writes epic fantasy fiction and more besides as Juliet E McKenna.

Also by J. M. Alvey

Shadows of Athens

Scorpions in Corinth

Justice for Athena

More dyslexic friendly

titles coming soon...

Lightning Source UK Ltd.
Milton Keynes UK
UKHW011230040922
408286UK00002B/58